AF270214

Pembroke Welsh Corgis

by Grace Hansen

Abdo Kids Jumbo is an Imprint of Abdo Kids
abdobooks.com

abdobooks.com

Published by Abdo Kids, a division of ABDO, P.O. Box 398166, Minneapolis, Minnesota 55439.
Copyright © 2022 by Abdo Consulting Group, Inc. International copyrights reserved in all countries.
No part of this book may be reproduced in any form without written permission from the publisher.
Abdo Kids Jumbo™ is a trademark and logo of Abdo Kids.

Printed in China

052021

092021

THIS BOOK CONTAINS RECYCLED MATERIALS

Photo Credits: Getty Images, iStock, Shutterstock, Thinkstock

Production Contributors: Teddy Borth, Jennie Forsberg, Grace Hansen
Design Contributors: Dorothy Toth, Pakou Moua

Library of Congress Control Number: 2020947623
Publisher's Cataloging-in-Publication Data

Names: Hansen, Grace, author.
Title: Pembroke welsh corgis / by Grace Hansen
Description: Minneapolis, Minnesota : Abdo Kids, 2022 | Series: Dogs | Includes online resources and
    index.
Identifiers: ISBN 9781098206031 (lib. bdg.) | ISBN 9781098206598 (ebook) | ISBN 9781098206871
    (Read-to-Me ebook)
Subjects: LCSH: Pembroke Welsh corgi--Juvenile literature. | Herding dogs--Juvenile literature. | Dogs--
    Juvenile literature. | Animal behavior--Juvenile literature.
Classification: DDC 599.772--dc23

Table of Contents

Pembroke Welsh Corgis

The Pembroke Welsh corgi

is from Pembrokeshire.

Pembrokeshire is in Wales, a

country in the United Kingdom.

United Kingdom
Wales
Europe
N
W
E
S

The Pembroke corgi's **roots** go back to the early 1100s. It was then that two kinds of dogs were brought to Wales. From them, the Pembroke corgi was **bred**.

Pembroke corgis were **bred** to work on farms. They were trained to herd birds like geese and chickens. They could also rid farms of rats and other pests.

Corgis could also herd larger animals, like pigs and cattle. The dogs would nip at the animals' heels. Their short height helped them avoid being kicked.

Pembroke corgis are small and **sturdy**. They stand just 10 to 12 inches (25-30 cm) tall. They weigh around 30 pounds (14 kg).

Pembroke corgis have pointed ears. Their tails are docked. Their legs are short but powerful.

Their coats are medium in
length. They can be red, **sable**,
fawn, black, or tan in color.
They can have white markings.

Exercise

Corgis need exercise every day. Daily walks and play are important. They also need firm but kind training.

Personality

Corgis are smart and strong willed. They are also loving without being too needy. The dog's fun personality and cheerful face make owning one fun!

More Facts

- Queen Elizabeth II's favorite pups in the world are Pembroke Welsh corgis. She has owned more than 30 in her lifetime.

- Though both called corgis, the Pembroke Welsh corgi and the Cardigan Welsh corgi are two separate **breeds**.

- Pembrokes are good watch dogs. They will bark if anyone or anything comes near their homes.

Glossary

bred – developed over time for a certain purpose.

breed – a particular type of animal.

docked – shortened.

fawn – yellowish tan.

roots – family background.

sable – very dark.

sturdy – strong, hardy, or solid.

Index

Visit **abdokids.com** to access crafts, games, videos, and more!